398.2   Stanley, Diane.
STA

        Petrosinella.

                          33722000140004
             $14.89   06/23/1995

001217   11-111-11   ˈ39382

PETROSINELLA

PETROSINELLA
A NEAPOLITAN RAPUNZEL

RETOLD AND ILLUSTRATED BY
DIANE STANLEY

DIAL BOOKS FOR YOUNG READERS

NEW YORK

For

PETER,

a real prince

Published by Dial Books for Young Readers
A Division of Penguin Books USA Inc.
375 Hudson Street
New York, New York 10014

Designed by Julie Rauer
Printed in Hong Kong
First Edition
1 3 5 7 9 10 8 6 4 2

Library of Congress Cataloging in Publication Data
Stanley, Diane.
Petrosinella: a Neapolitan Rapunzel/retold and
illustrated by Diane Stanley. — 1st ed.
p. cm.
Summary: In this version of Rapunzel, the heroine breaks the
enchantment put on her by the ogress who keeps
her prisoner with the aid of three acorns.
ISBN 0-8037-1712-1 (trade)—ISBN 0-8037-1714-8 (library).
[1. Fairy tales. 2. Folklore — Italy.] I. Basile, Giambattista,
ca. 1575–1632. Petrosinella. English. II. Title.
PZ8. S483Pe 1995 398.2'0945'7302 — dc20 [E]94-17456 CIP AC

The artwork is rendered in watercolor and colored inks.

The illustrations in this book first appeared in an edition
of *Petrosinella* published by Frederick Warne & Co. Inc. in 1981.

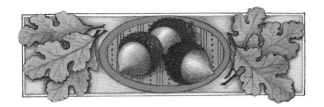

The story of *Petrosinella* has much in common with the Grimm story *Rapunzel*—but it was recorded nearly two hundred years before the Brothers Grimm published their tales. *Petrosinella* appeared in what may be the earliest collection of European fairy stories in existence: *The Pentamerone* of Giambattista Basile, published in 1637. The fifty stories in *The Pentamerone* came directly from the oral tradition at such an early date that Jacob Grimm called them "the wonderful, last echoes of very ancient myths which have taken root over the whole of Europe."

This important book is unfamiliar to us because it was written in the Neapolitan dialect, an archaic and difficult language. Over the next three hundred and fifty years a few brave souls attempted to translate it, but with no dictionaries to guide them, they often fell into error. For this retelling I consulted several English translations, including the 1847 version by John Edward Taylor and the more recent translation by N.M. Penzer, published in 1932. This latter book, which is by far the best, was first translated from Neapolitan into Italian in 1925 by the great scholar and philosopher Benedetto Croce. Later Penzer gave it to us in English.

In his preface Penzer says that his book is "intended for the select few—for scholars and students of sociology, folk-lore and storiology." This, however, is a book for children, and in retelling the story I have made some minor changes to add psychological realism, logic, and clarity. For example, in the original the mother hands her daughter over to the ogress without a fight, merely because she is tired of being reminded of her promise. In my version the mother is outwitted by the ogress, who takes the girl by force.

Most of the story appears here unchanged, including Petrosinella's famous long, golden hair and the device of the magic acorns. They are a noteworthy and, I feel, welcome departure from *Rapunzel* in giving the heroine a more active role in her escape and in her subsequent happiness.   D.S.

Once upon a time there was a woman who lived next door to an ogress. The ogress had a large garden where she grew beautiful flowers and every kind of herb, but the garden was hidden behind a high wall and a locked door. Now, the woman could see over the wall from her upstairs window, and she often looked longingly into the garden. She was expecting a child, and perhaps that is why she developed such a fierce craving for the rich, green parsley that grew in big bunches down below.

One day the ogress went out, carefully locking the door behind her. As the woman watched her go, she thought how easy it would be to climb over the wall and take some of the parsley. After all, she thought to herself, there is so much—the ogress will never miss it.

The parsley tasted so wonderful that the woman could not get enough of it. Day after day she waited for the ogress to leave the house, then crept into the garden and helped herself. After a while the ogress began to suspect that it wasn't just birds who were eating her parsley. She decided to find out who it was that dared to steal from her garden.

The next day she went out as usual, only this time she came back quickly. And sure enough, there she found the woman, still clutching a bunch of parsley in her hand.

"Thief!" roared the ogress. "You shall die for this!" With that she rushed at the terrified woman as if to kill her on the spot.

"Oh, have mercy," begged the woman. "Do not kill me over such a little thing. Please let me pay you for what I have taken. I will give you anything!"

"Anything?" asked the ogress. "Is that a promise?"

"Oh, yes," said the woman, "if you will let me live."

"Then you must give me your child when it is born, whether it be a boy or a girl. Now go, and do not come back!"

Soon afterward the woman gave birth to a beautiful baby girl, and on her little chest was a birthmark in the shape of a delicate sprig of parsley. That is why the woman called her daughter Petrosinella, which meant parsley.

Seven years passed, and the woman was so perfectly happy with her little girl that she stopped worrying about her promise to the ogress. Surely the horrible creature had forgotten!

Then one day Petrosinella was walking by the garden door on her way to school. She had passed it many times before, and it was always locked. But on that day the door suddenly opened, and a hideous old woman emerged and spoke to her.

"Your mother promised me something years ago," growled the ogress. "Today I am going to take it."

And with that she took the frightened child into the deepest part of a dense forest. There, by magic, the ogress made a tower rise far above the tallest tree. Then she took Petrosinella up a dark, winding stairway to a little room at the top that had only one window, sealing the door behind them so the child could not get out.

Now, Petrosinella had beautiful golden hair, and the ogress had taken a fancy to it. With one of her magic spells she made it grow and grow, until it was so long that when the child leaned out the window, her hair reached all the way to the ground. And whenever the ogress wanted to come or go from the tower, she would use Petrosinella's long hair as a ladder.

In that tower Petrosinella spent her childhood and grew to be a young woman. Her only comfort was to stand at the window and gaze out on a world that she could never enter. She would spend hours there, feeling the warmth of the sun on her face, and singing to pass the time.

One day, when the ogress was away, a prince came riding through the forest, and he happened to hear her lovely voice carried on the wind. He was so enchanted by the sound that he searched everywhere for the singer, until he found Petrosinella's tower. Looking up, he saw her at the window, gazing down on him, and her beauty took his breath away.

"Oh, please," he called up to her, "won't you come down?"

"I cannot," she answered, "but you can come to me." And she let down her long golden hair.

When he reached the little room at the top of the tower, he grasped Petrosinella's hands and gazed at her in amazement. For though he had seen the greatest beauties in the land, none of those fine ladies had ever touched his heart as had this mysterious girl.

Petrosinella knew nothing of the world. Since childhood she had seen the face of no living soul except her dreadful captor. Yet she had a wise heart, and she knew that this young man, who looked upon her with such tenderness, was the one she would love forever.

Still, she begged him to go. "I am kept here by a wicked ogress," she told him, "and she must not find you here!"

"Then I will go now, but I will come back when the moon has risen. Put some poppy juice in her soup," he said, "and she will sleep so deeply, she will not hear a thing."

Petrosinella did as the prince suggested, and so that night, and many nights afterward, he returned in the safety of darkness. While the ogress slept, they told one another all the important things—their memories and fears and hopes. Night after night they talked and laughed and fell more and more in love.

One evening the prince left the tower as he always did, well before dawn, believing that no one had seen him. But he was mistaken, for there was a nosy old witch, a friend of the ogress, who often came to the forest by moonlight to find mushrooms and herbs for her spells. It happened that she was there that evening and she saw him. The next day the witch paid a visit to the tower.

"If you are not careful," said the witch in a low voice, "your little bird will fly away." And she told the ogress what she had seen.

"Ah," said the ogress with a nasty grin, "but I have clipped my little bird's wings. I have cast a spell on her, and she can never, ever leave her perch." Then she bent closer to the witch and told her a secret: There was only one charm that could break the spell. "It's three magic acorns," she whispered, "and you'll never guess where I hid them—in the rafters!"

They shared a good laugh over that. But Petrosinella, standing quietly behind a curtain, smiled too—for she had heard every word.

That night when the prince came, she told him about the magic acorns. Quickly he climbed onto a chair and began to search the rafters. He found the acorns easily and gave them to Petrosinella, who put them in her pocket. Then they set about tearing up the sheets and bedcovers to make a rope, and soon they made their escape.

But as luck would have it, the nosy witch was there again that night. Seeing them escape, she let out such a racket of shrieking and roaring that the ogress awoke with a start.

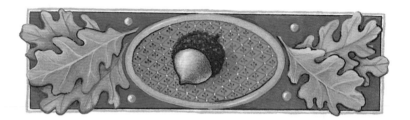

The ogress hurried down the rope ladder and set off after the lovers. Racing like the wind, she was soon at their heels.

When Petrosinella saw the ogress, she was paralyzed by terror. But then she remembered the acorns. Surely such powerful charms could save her now! Taking one from her pocket, she flung it at the ogress. And suddenly, where the acorn had fallen, there stood a ferocious dog, poised to attack the ogress with savage jaws and murderous, sharp teeth.

But the ogress was not so easily defeated. Like a flash, she brought forth a loaf of bread and threw it at the dog. Instantly it grew tame and began gobbling down the bread, as timid as a squirrel. Again the ogress took up the chase.

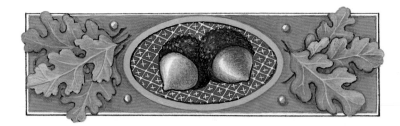

As she and the prince raced down the road, Petrosinella heard the sound of rapid footsteps behind them. They were still in danger! She took out the second acorn and threw it at the ogress.

This time a great shaggy lion appeared. With a low growl deep in its throat, it began to stalk the old woman.

But now the ogress used her magic to produce the hide of a donkey, and threw it over herself. At this mysterious transformation the lion was puzzled, and crept away in search of a less changeable meal. Now, for the third time, the ogress set off after the young couple.

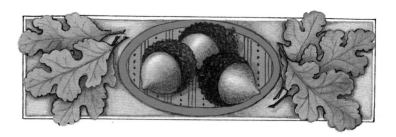

When she heard the sound of heavy footsteps coming yet again, Petrosinella despaired of ever defeating the dreadful creature. With her last hope of escape, Petrosinella threw down the final acorn. From its magic arose a ferocious wolf. It did not take time to show its teeth or growl. In a heartbeat it fell upon the ogress. This time when they ran away, no one followed.

And so they came, at last, to the palace. No sooner had they arrived than they began to plan their wedding. Only one thing was lacking to make their happiness complete: A messenger was sent to fetch Petrosinella's grieving mother. And how joyful the poor woman was to find her child, lost for so many years, and on the very next day to see her become a princess.

After that they put away all thought of sorrows past,
and made every day a blessing for as long as they lived.